ABOUT THE BOOK

It seemed like the perfect crime… that should have been his first warning.

Labor Day Weekend, an empty office building down in sleepy Point Loma: basically a sitting-duck target for any second-story man worth a nickel. Especially one with a lifetime of skills to draw upon—not to mention all the magic passcodes tucked comfortably away in his back pocket.

Nothing could go wrong, or that was how it seemed… but in the end, he couldn't honestly blame anyone but himself for not seeing it coming.

From **A. J. Payler**, author of *The Killing Song, Bank Error in Your Favor,* and *Terror Next Door* comes **Default Admin Credentials**, a story of struggle against overwhelming odds and unstoppable fear.

Also featuring bonus story **Dictated, Never Read** (as seen in *Twenty-two Twenty-eight*)!

OTHER BOOKS BY A. J. PAYLER

BANK ERROR IN YOUR FAVOR

What would you do if enough money to solve all your problems fell in your lap?

Shane and Jewel have been hanging onto the edges of life by their fingernails for so long, they can't remember any other way of living. When enough money to solve all their problems drops out of the sky, it seems like a windfall from heaven—but it might be the worst thing that could ever have happened.

Can love survive when money comes between lovers? Caught between the criminal underground and the law, Shane and Jewel race towards freedom despite a parade of bizarre characters, secret plans, and hidden agendas standing between them and the life they so desperately need. And worst of all, their greatest enemy of all might be looking back at them from the mirror—or right by their side.

https://books2read.com/bankerror

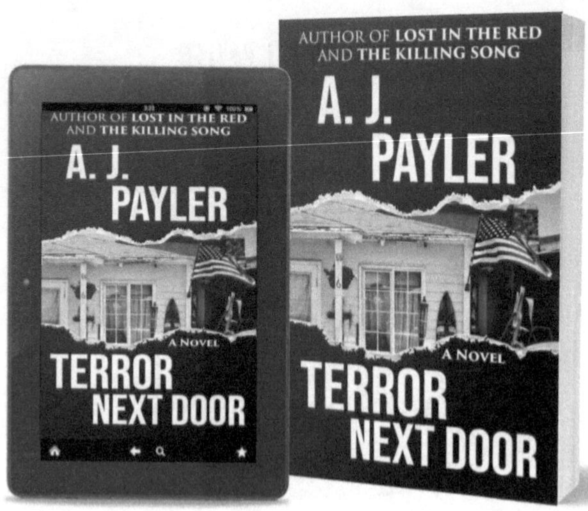

TERROR NEXT DOOR

**Quarantined. Isolated. Paranoid.
TRAPPED.**

Stuck at home with nowhere to run, Kevin Tamura isn't holding up well under quarantine.

Exhausted from overwork and lack of sleep, his sanity slips as society crumbles.

But what will he do to protect himself when the greatest terror of all might be hiding right next door?

From the mind of A. J. Payler, author of *Lost In the Red* and *The Killing Song*, comes a story of a man pushed to the edge in a world that's ready to break.

Suffused with gripping tension, the explosive TERROR NEXT DOOR is a thrilling suspense novel no reader will ever forget.

https://books2read.com/terrornextdoor

Lost In the Red

Out of their element—and trapped beyond time!

Carson Adkins had no doubt he was born unlucky, especially after his college folded one semester before graduation—but he never expected to find himself caught deep in the heart of an uncharted land sheltered against the passage of time for decades!

Compelled to struggle for survival against terrifying odds and unfamiliar threats, Carson finds himself in a world he never expected, where every encounter forces him to confront deadly opponents and difficult truths.

When the alluring Delilah Munson joins his journey, Carson believes he may finally have discovered something worth fighting for—but as he soon discovers, this opaque backwoods jewel has her own agenda, not to mention the will to carry it out.

Torn between two worlds, can the fragile yet ever-growing attraction between a rural princess and a modern man far from home possibly survive in the face of a cataclysmic conflict far beyond the bounds of anything either could ever have imagined?

The Killing Song.
A NOVEL
A. J. PAYLER
The Killing Song.
A NOVEL
A. J. PAYLER
The Killing Song.
A NOVEL
J. PAYLER

Get a free story when you sign up for the newsletter

Sign up for the A. J. Payler newsletter at http://ajpayler.com now to get the short story "Sonata of Fear" sent directly to you immediately, as well as receive future notifications of new releases.

Your email will not be shared with any other organizations or individuals, and you will not be barraged with marketing nonsense. Feel free to unsubscribe or resubscribe at any time; no one's feelings will be hurt. (Also, maybe check your junk/spam folder if you don't see the subscription confirmation with your free download link pop up relatively quickly.)

DEFAULT ADMIN CREDENTIALS

+bonus story "Dictated, Never Read"

A. J. PAYLER

CONTENTS

DEFAULT ADMIN CREDENTIALS

People argue about how complex passwords should be. But the truth is, it makes a lot less of a difference how a password is changed than whether anyone ever actually bothers to get around to changing it.

Most people would be amazed to know what percentage of computer systems never get their passwords changed. It changes from industry to industry, but not as much as you'd think, hovering somewhere between a third and a half across the board, even in high-tech fields where the people involved should—and definitely do— know better.

Kind of shocking, right? Routers, switches, mainframes, entire networks. Pretty much any and every crucial piece of the entire telecommunications backbone, basically all running on the default credentials they shipped with for years at a time.

And these default admin credentials, the magic passwords that let anyone access and mess around with the guts and internal working of the thing, you can look them

up online without ever having to buy a piece of equipment. Check it out for yourself.

So if you do your homework and you can find out the
make and manufacture of any given system, you have a
damn fair shot at a butter-smooth entry without even a
whiff of risk. It doesn't matter much whether a company
manufactures soft drinks, builds military kit, or designs
networking technology, if you can find out what make of
equipment they use and finagle a means of uninterrupted
access to said equipment, at least half the time plugging in
the preconfigured default setup password will give you
full admin privileges.

The best part is, ninety-nine-point-nine percent of the
time you can count on the fact that the type of person who
doesn't bother changing their passwords on one system
never bothers to change their passwords anywhere. So
once you find a viable target, it's generally safe to assume
whatever systems they have access to are similarly unde-
fended: security cameras, alarms, even personal email.
'Hacking' a password like you see in the movies and on
television—random guessing at birthdays, hobbies, childhood pets, even unconnected objects around the room—is
never necessary and doesn't work like that anyway,
because someone too lazy to change the admin keypass for
their multi-thousand security system is the same person
who keeps their computer login on a sticky note under the
keyboard.

If you're one of these people, take solace in the fact that
you shouldn't blame yourself. It's just human nature, and
believe me, you aren't alone by a long shot. We all imagine
our friends, neighbors, and enemies are vigilant about
keeping responsible practices, but for the most part they're
all just like you.

Anyway, all this is taking the long way to getting

around to explaining how I ended up in the situation I got myself into this Labor Day weekend.

The Wiltshire Building is a squat, ungainly three-story painted slate gray, situated on the corner of a couple of glorified back alleys down in the industrial section of San Diego's Point Loma neighborhood. Point Loma itself is a peninsula, so access in and out of the place is limited to a couple of major roads and traffic tends to slow to a crawl whenever anything of note happens there—which is why I thought an overcast Labor Day would be the perfect time to finally get around to breaking into the offices of Carillion Industries, a four-room arrangement on the Wiltshire Building's second floor. A day with no business meant no traffic, no interruptions, and no risk. In and out in an hour or less and no one gets hurt, least of all me. It seemed perfect.

Unfortunately, that's not the way it worked.

Oh, I got past the office building security system without a hitch—it was old and unpatched and vulnerable to about seven different strategies—and rode the elevator straight up to Carillion's front door. Their keypad was a different make than that of the building itself but offered no greater challenge, so I was in their lobby within five minutes and had their security cameras shut down within ten.

For the next half-hour I scrounged through the front of the Carillion offices, ball cap screwed down tight on my head to keep from leaving any stray hairs for the authorities to test my DNA and shade my face from any backup cameras I might have missed, latex gloves keeping my fingerprints from any of the surfaces I touched, sunglasses on to hide my eye color and so forth. You know, the usual routine.

A couple of petty cash boxes scavenged from bottom

desk drawers added up to about five thousand in legal tender stuffed into the pockets of my workman's jumpsuit —always dress like you might have some legitimate excuse to be on the property, plus a jumpsuit covers a lot of potentially identifying marks—so I was pretty happy with the day's take before even getting into the back offices.

What I should have done at that point was to cut my losses, turned around and left both the office and building and driven right the fuck out of Point Loma right then. I would have been coming out five grand ahead and run almost zero risk of being caught.

But then I turned a corner, looked through a thick glass door and realized that behind the expansive black walnut desk in the CEO's office, there was a safe set into the wall.

And not just any random wall safe, but a Kroll-Siemens 480, recognizable by its distinctive hexagonal profile. Infamous in certain circles for its many, many design flaws, which made it only slightly more protection than just leaving your valuables in a mound in the middle of the floor.

Now, in retrospect, I should have been suspicious there was nothing obscuring the face of the safe, piece of junk or not. I mean, even the dumbest uppity prick hangs a self-aggrandizing portrait or a blowup of their boat or some ugly painting he paid too much for on the wall to conceal a safe, right? But okay, I missed that in my zeal to find out just what that Kroll-Siemens 480 might contain. No one could blame me for that.

The same admin passkey that opened the Carillion front office door unlocked the touchpad protecting the CEO's inner sanctum, no muss no fuss. Before you could say payday, I had my ear pressed to the safe, tapping around its edges to see what she had to tell me. And baby, it was a lot—this model hadn't even been upgraded in accordance with the recall Kroll-Siemens was forced to send out after the depths of their incompetence became known. That meant all it would take to pop the door was a flathead screwdriver applied in just the right spot, and the multi-tool I always kept hooked to my belt while on the job gave me three different flatheads on command.

So here's the thing: in my line of work, if you get past three different security hurdles to get access to a thing without trouble, that tends to set a pattern, right? It lulls you into a state of arrogance, like you can do whatever you want to people too stupid to take the most basic precautions to protect themselves.

You get lazy, is what I'm saying. And that's what happened here.

I mean, some rich asshole has a nonupgraded Kroll-Siemens 480 set into his wall, to me and others like me that's just asking to be robbed. And I guess that's what the idea was there, now that I put it all together: to create the image of an irresistible target, paint the picture of a sitting duck, in such a way that only a person with my specialized knowledge would recognize it. And why would anyone do something like that? The only reason would be to draw that person in.

I recall thinking, just before popping the face off the safe, that I had no idea what the hell business Carillion Industries was even in. Real estate? Bail bonds? Financial services? Who the hell knew? The name was vague enough that it could imply anything and everything or nothing at all, all at the same time.

I wasn't even sure how the place had gotten on my radar, not entirely. There are a few deep web bulletin boards where people like me buy, sell, and trade information about potential jobs, targets, and the like, so chances were solid I must have run across it there.

But I knew I hadn't paid for the tip, so it couldn't have been too carefully vetted. These websites are obscure, sure, but I don't fool myself they're secure enough that the cops and other miscreants don't know about them.

As I applied pressure with my multi-tool, I felt the face of the safe about to give way. The muscles in my shoulders tensed unconsciously, bracing for the piercing squeal of an alarm as it popped loose and came off in my hands—but there was nothing.

I grinned, tossing the face aside carelessly. With the entire guts of the lock mechanism exposed, even a toddler could open the thing in less than a minute; just click the tumblers into place, turn the handle, and blammo. That was why Kroll-Siemens paid out big bucks in their settlement, that was why anyone who was serious about trying to protect their belongings had long since gone back for the upgrade.

I was no toddler, so I had the door wide in a few seconds.

As I reached my hand inside, the hairs on the back of my neck stood on end. I shrugged it off as the thrill of the moment, the excitement of the hunt.

That wasn't it at all though, I now realize. It was my instincts, screaming at their lungs to try to warn me off at the last minute. Too late.

My fingers tripped some kind of laser sensor—or heat sensor, or movement sensor, one of those—situated inside the safe. Now, such a thing isn't unheard of, but in a place sloppy enough to have default credentials as issued on all their systems and a piece of crap wall safe? No one would expect it there.

I certainly didn't. And that's what they were counting on.

The office door behind me slammed shut with a hydraulic crash, a battery of resolute thunks signaling deadbolts sliding home into the walls all around me: the door, the windows, even the drawers of the desk itself. All secured firmly, with me still standing there with my hand in the otherwise empty safe and my dick in my hand, figuratively speaking.

My chin sagged to my chest, and I knew I was caught.

For the next half hour I checked and double-checked and triple-checked every opening, every lock, every crevice, from the sealed industrial triple-pane windows to the two-inch diameter ventilation shafts to the less than sixteenth-inch gap between door and threshold. I even pulled off the electrical plates, probing around the walls for weak spots in the drywall.

But in my heart I knew I wouldn't find anything, no matter how hard I looked. Mostly I just had to satisfy myself because I wouldn't have been able to forgive myself for not trying if I hadn't at least made the attempt.

But as expected, my search came up empty. There was no way out of this room, and I had the expertise to know that for certain as an irrefutable fact, as sure as up was up and down was down.

That was how they caught me, playing to that knowledge. When the mind knows a thing, it yearns to exercise that knowledge, to show off what it knows, try to distinguish itself above the pack. It's just human nature.

And there, trapped alone in the aridity of that solitary office with nothing to do but think, it came to me where the Carillion info came to me from. It was in a file I kept on my laptop in my apartment, containing information I'd dug up and cobbled together—and yes, sometimes even paid for—regarding potential targets, jobs I might undertake in the future. You can't just rely on waiting for things to drop in your lap, not if you want to maintain any semblance of a regular cash flow. You never know when you might need a bunch of money all of a sudden, after all. So a guy in my position has to always be tossing around somewhere between a few and a few dozen possibilities.

I didn't consciously recall putting that Carillion data in there, but I guess I must have assumed I copied it in there late one night after having a few strong double IPAs and tossing back a few gummies. It wouldn't be the first time I woke up to information in my job file I didn't consciously remember putting in there, though admittedly most of that type of info usually turned out to be irrelevant garbage.

Now, what I think is someone planted that information there to lure me. Knowing it would float to the top of my queue by presenting a target too tempting to resist. Or at least for a guy like me to resist.

I couldn't help kicking myself. All I would have had to do to prevent this would have been to change the default admin credentials on my laptop, the way I had on my modem and router. One weak link in the chain, one tiny oversight, and I was lost.

Now, I have no options left to me but to sit here slumped in this not-as-plush-as-it-looks office chair, staring out the unbreakable windows waiting for the blinding San Diego sun to come up, all the while wondering what type of person whoever eventually comes to get me might be, and what someone smart enough to pull this off could possibly want with a guy like me.

My guess is, there's no way it's anything good.

It was a beautiful Sunday morning, shimmering rays of perfect golden sunlight reflecting placidly off the as-yet unbroken surface of the isolated mountain lake. The owls and chittering insects of the night had already retreated to their dens, all the night's hunters bedded down, relinquishing the day to the flora and fauna of morning—a decidedly more peaceful, soothing time.

Aerendyl Kiyama stretched her willowy limbs as her burnt umber eyelids fluttered open, greeting the arrival of the day—but not just any day, no. This was a special day, the day of her oh for fucksake you dumb asshole, please do the rest of us the favor of paying just the slightest bit of attention where you're going.

Oh Jesus, now look at this prick. Just take all day why don't you, it's not like anyone has anywhere to be at seven oh three on a Monday, yes surely we're all just cruising around downtown gawking at the skyscrapers like we just fell off the turnip truck and have never seen buildings taller than three stories before.

Yes yes, I see you, just move out of the way please.

All right, fucking finally. Where the shit was I? Oh right, the day of reckoning. So yeah, um, not just any day, this day of reckoning was one Aerendyl knew without a doubt she would ah, fuck! Jesus that's hot, where the hell are those napkins I stuffed down the console for emergencies just like this?

Ow ow ow ow ow. Oh man, this skirt is ruined. I knew wearing this shade of beige was a mistake on a day like today. Look at that, that's gonna sting later. And just great, now I don't have any coffee left either. Lovely.

So. Right. This day was one that would decide her future, to finally resolve whether Aerendyl would be allowed to pursue the path of the warrior—a desire all knew had long burned in her breast, to avenge the untimely death of her older brother Raloto—or if she would be consigned to the distaff lodge, there to dedicate herself to the perfection of the domestic arts.

Aerendyl shuddered, knowing she would be a different person by the time night again fell and the hunters of the forest roamed once more. Or would she, in fact, be the person she always had been as well as the person she was always meant to be?

Oh, what is this now. Ugh, are you serious? Fine, fine, pick up. Pick up!

Hello. What is it?

No, really, mother—I'm on my way to the office, I don't —all right, all right, fine. Good morning. How are you. I am fine. Now, what is it?

Oh, please. You call out of the blue during literally the only nineteen minutes of time I have to myself the entire f-ing day and then you dither around, I'm sorry, but yes, I'm going to tend to be blunt. I apologize.

Now will you please tell me why you—oh.

Well, why didn't you—no, I see.

Yes, I'm sorry, I'm sorry, I already said—yes, of course, I will.

Okay. Yes. Okay. I'll talk to you later.

Bye, mom. I love you.

Fuck.

Um. Aerendyl, um, Aerendyl stared at the water. It, um.

Fuck.

ALSO BY A. J. PAYLER

NOVELS:

The Killing Song

World of Heroes: The Untold Secret Origin of the New Fighters

Lost In the Red

Terror Next Door

Bank Error In Your Favor

NONFICTION:

Trapped in This World: Culture on the Edge—The Omnibus of
Pop Culture Writing

Encore: The Anthology of Music Writing

ALBUMS (AS AARON POEHLER):

20th Century Gold - Juvenilia

This Is My Revenge

You Had To Leave Your Mark

Dietrich

That Says It All

Born to multiracial heritage in the same Honolulu hospital as Barack Obama, A. J. Payler earned his English degree from the University of Hawai'i, then eked out a living variously as a musician, technical writer, radio broadcaster, military contractor, audio engineer, comic store clerk, short order cook, press clipping agent, music journalist, and congressional archival assistant, shaking hands with everyone from Motörhead's Lemmy to Kurt Vonnegut along the way.

Since turning his attention to writing full-time, he has released the novels *The Killing Song*, *World of Heroes: The Untold Secret Origin of the New Fighters*, *Lost In the Red*, *Terror Next Door*, and *Bank Error In Your Favor*; his short writing has been published by Suspect, Twenty-Two Twenty-Eight, Flipside, Songwriter's Market, Creepy podcast, Cloaked Press, Short Story (Substack), EYE, Tailspins, Razorcake and more. He has also recorded and released several well-reviewed albums of original songs and opened for artists such as Silkworm and the Schizophonics, continuing to perform live as often as time permits.

He lives in Southern California with his family. Further detail on his writing and music is available via http://linktr.ee/ajpayler and http://ajpayler.com, where readers can get sign up for the A. J. Payler newsletter to hear about new releases and get free stories as they're released.

Aaron Poehler
THAT SAYS IT ALL
DIETRICH

20th CENTURY GOLD
AARON POEHLER
The Juvenilia Collection

BONUS SAMPLE CHAPTERS: BANK ERROR IN YOUR FAVOR

Chapters 1 and 2

CHAPTER ONE

TUESDAY, APRIL 4, 2017
BETHLEHEM, INDIANA

As he shut the alarm off just before the clock ticked over to six a.m., Shane wondered how much longer he and Jewel could manage to keep going the way they had been.

A month, maybe two? And that was if they were lucky, which they weren't.

Shane had known he wasn't a lucky man for a long time. Sometimes, he thought everyone around him knew it too. And on the few occasions he had dared to think differently, the inevitabilities of life had a way of showing him the error of his ways.

Take the night he'd met Jewel, for example: in that moment when he'd first seen her, he vividly recalled thinking that his luck must have turned. Why else would a girl that hot be smiling at him? It certainly wasn't for anything he'd done; Shane went to bars to drink, not to hit on women. His face had received more than enough slaps over the years to train him well in that regard.

And yet, here was this dark-haired beauty giving off every sign of believing Shane looked like the best catch in the place—and it wasn't even within spitting distance of closing time.

He'd actually glanced behind him to make sure she wasn't staring past him at someone more attractive, but no: she'd caught his self-conscious glance, smiled coyly, and beckoned him to her with a single crook of her finger. And against all odds, when he got to her table, she even had a full drink sitting on the table in front of her and an empty seat beside her.

The rest of the night was a blur, as he'd had a few drinks already before that point, but it was a happy blur. And the morning after had brought the biggest surprise of all when the dawning of the new day failed to disperse either the woman or her attractiveness. She'd stayed; they'd had breakfast; and to top it all off, the phone number she gave him actually reached her when he called it later in the day.

He'd never dared to ask Jewel what had first drawn her to him that night. But once Shane got to know her, he knew it didn't much matter: as long as she chose to be with him, he was fucked for good.

She was too pretty for him, and she knew it, and he knew it, and everyone who ever saw them together probably knew it—but he couldn't give her up. So every time she should have been well-rested but yawned regardless, he took it seriously: was she getting bored of him? Of them? Of who she was when she was with him?

After all, a girl that beautiful could be with anyone. If he didn't keep her interested, someone else surely would.

Worse, Jewel acted like anytime anyone else in the

world was winning, somehow that meant she was losing. And Jewel hated losing more than anything—more than her mother, even.

So ever since that day, Shane's life had felt like a race he couldn't win. Sooner or later, Jewel was bound to realize Shane couldn't keep up with her—and that day, his life would be over. He might keep walking along, his lungs might continue to process air, blood might keep flowing through his veins, but his heart would be gone forever.

Shane rubbed his bleary eyes, yawned, and looked over at her: still sleeping, of course. He hadn't heard her come in, but the bar didn't stop serving drinks until two a.m. And even though on Monday nights the tips barely added up to enough to make it worth keeping the doors open, closing early was anathema to its owner—as was kicking anyone out with even a swallow left in their glass. So it might easily have been three a.m. or later by the time she'd finally crawled into bed with him, at which point he was dead to the world.

Slipping gently from the covers and gingerly placing first one foot, then the other on the floor, Shane lifted a single Venetian blind with the tip of his finger and peered through, squinting.

Outside, all was still. Still, and dark. The birds that made their home in the massive oak that dominated their miniscule backyard weren't even chirping yet.

Shane stifled a groan and stepped lightly towards the bathroom, taking care not to disturb the snoozing Jewel. By the time she awoke, he'd be halfway through his workday; by the time he got home, she'd be preparing to head off for her own shift.

Lately, it seemed that they saw each other only in passing. Even weekends were rarely a guarantee of time to reconnect—because Jewel's weekend shifts tended to pay the best, they were the hardest for her to turn down, even taking into account the elevated chances of her getting pawed by intoxicated customers.

Shane's breath escaped in a burst through gritted teeth as he shut the bathroom door behind him, his eyelids nearly closed against the glare of the buzzing fluorescent bulb overhead. Knowing the ancient pipes in their tiny rented house would take forever to ferry heated water to the shower, he turned the water on before sinking onto the toilet seat, one hand supporting his weary head while the other propped his phone directly before his eyes, its thumb swiping aimlessly from app to app in search of distraction.

As usual, the headlines of the day made little impact on his consciousness. Shane tended to consider most newsworthy issues far enough above his pay grade that his opinions on such matters would almost certainly never be of the slightest importance to anyone, himself included.

And apparently none of the people he was connected to on social media had anything of interest to declare, either. Not yet, anyway; few rose as early in the day as Shane was forced to.

Sighing, he clicked over to his email with reluctance. While national feeds rarely conveyed good news and social media did so only slightly more often, of late any and all news coming to him through email had seemed to be uniformly bad.

And sure enough, immediately after refreshing his inbox, a bold, all-caps subject line fairly leaped out at him: "IMPORTANT NOTICE: ACCOUNT OVERDRAWN."

"Aw, fuck me twice," Shane muttered to no one in particular as he stood and flushed the toilet. He must've miscalculated the timing of one or more of their bill debits hitting the account somehow, or maybe a check had taken longer than expected to clear. Whatever had caused the issue, after bringing up his checking account the problem glowed out at him in vivid red text: "Balance: -$19.43".

Shane knew from hard-won experience that there was little sense in worrying about the specifics just then, since most customer service departments wouldn't be open for at least another hour. Even if they had been, jabbering away trying to explain away the situation would be sure to annoy Jewel as she slept—it wasn't like their house was big enough for him to get away anywhere his voice wouldn't carry. And something about those customer service reps and their smarmy, superior tones always got to him, to the point that somehow he always found himself shouting down the line, desperately trying to get them to understand his problem, to do whatever was in their limited power to do to help him, for fucksake.

And in any case, it wasn't like he could just transfer money from another account to cover the threadbare checking, anyway. Whatever solution he'd eventually be forced to cobble together would likely involve substantial concessions on his part, rigorously defined payment plans he'd probably be unable to keep up with, and—almost certainly—a hearty dose of humiliation.

Therefore, at the moment there was nothing else to be done but to hang his head, resign himself to the beginning of the workday, and jump into the shower for a last few minutes of warm, womblike comfort, utterly silent outside of the rushing of the water—the sole benefit he'd been able to identify to rising so early in the morning.

"Eee-yiii, holy fuck," Shane shouted before he was able to stop himself. "God damn it!" The water was arctic; he knew logically it couldn't literally be freezing cold, but it sure didn't feel far from it.

He spun the hot water handle left, then right, to no

avail: it was on as wide as it would go, and even with the cold tap completely shut off, the water temperature varied not a degree.

"Are you okay? Did you hurt yourself again?"

Shane flinched at Jewel's voice ringing out from the other room, more weary than concerned.

"Uh, sure," he sputtered. "I mean, no, I'm fine."

"Then what's all the racket?"

"It's, uh, it's the shower. There's no hot water."

The deep sigh she emitted seemed to speak volumes in reply, as did the barely concealed subtext of the questions that followed in its wake: "Did you pay it? On time? Like I told you?"

"Yeah, I did. I thought I did." He glanced back at his phone sitting atop the toilet tank. "They must have fucked up the account somehow."

"Uh-huh, I'm sure that's it," she muttered, her tone clearly indicating a lack of confidence in Shane's assertion. "Well, no matter what happened, I'm definitely going to need a shower before work this evening, so I'd appreciate if you could manage to get it unfucked as soon as possible."

"All right, baby, I'll try. Just go back to sleep."

"If I can with you shouting around all over the damn place," she mumbled, pulling the pillow over her head before he could reply.

Shane rolled his eyes, knowing she would be snoring again within moments.

He turned and nearly jumped in fright at the sight of his own face staring back at him from the mirror: haunted. Haunted, that's the word for how he looked, deep bags under his eyes, his cheeks unshaven, his hair thinning and receding more than it should for his age.

He groaned deeply, lifting the stopper into place and

turning the sink on to run an ice-cold basin of sudsy water. Ten minutes in and this day's already shot to hell, Shane thought, dipping his damp washcloth into the frigid water to clean himself up as best he could.

As he steered his shuddering green Ford Aspire into the parking lot at work, already eight minutes past the hour, Shane could faintly smell his musty armpits.

You never really notice how efficient a shower is at getting you clean until you have to do without, he mused to himself. He hoped his aroma wouldn't prompt any complaints from his co-workers, never inclined to suffer even minor indignities at the best of times.

Considering the odds, he decided he'd be best off going straight to the boss before anyone else had a chance. Besides, he had to talk to Dean, anyway.

Head down, he shouldered the glass lobby door open, inhaling deeply of the stale, overconditioned air. The perfectly made-up receptionist sipping a six-dollar cinnamon latte behind her desk didn't even bother to look up once as Shane typed his employee passcode into the security door keypad, and again, then a third time. Of course, she could have buzzed him in at any time, but that would require Shane not only managing to tear her attention from her phone, but getting her to concede that she recognized him.

On his fourth attempt, the keypad finally accepted Shane's code with a satisfied beep, followed by a buzzer to indicate he could pass. Shane felt his blood rise in his throat at the sly smile the receptionist permitted herself, but he could hardly defend himself after mistyping a four-digit passcode three times in a row. At least he hadn't hit five faulty entries that morning, which would not only have necessitated asking for her smirking assistance but requesting his passcode be manually reset. And considering the task with which he was already forced to begin his workday, any argument against his efficacy as an employee would have been less than desirable, no matter how seemingly inconsequential.

After taking a deep breath to steady his rattled nerves, Shane wiped the beads of sweat from his brow, smoothed his hair down, and shuffled down the worn gray industrial carpeting paving the hallway to his supervisor's office.

All around him, the sound of fingers on keyboards slowed in anticipation of a potentially entertaining scene to distract from the drudgery of the workday. Dean, he could see, was already peering through his open door, his long blond ponytail swinging behind him as he craned his neck to catch Shane's attention, no doubt alerted by the sound of his approaching footsteps. Dean's blue eyes seemingly gleamed and glittered at the prospect of a fresh opportunity to demean one of his charges, his pinstriped short-sleeve button-down shirt already speckled with crumbs of what looked like one of the glazed cake donuts made fresh by the place on the corner every morning.

"Ah, Shane! So good of you to join us this morning, and only twelve minutes past the hour. To what do we owe the privilege?"

"Sorry, Dean," Shane mumbled. "It's been a shitty morning all around."

"Mm," Dean answered through a mouthful of donut. "I hear you there. I mean, what's the point of even offering donuts with sprinkles if they're all going to be sold out by the time anyone gets a crack at them other than cops? They must know that same damned woman comes in and wipes them out of their whole stock every day."

He gestured with disgust at the half-eaten donut sitting on a square white napkin atop his desk. "The least they could do is to make enough to compensate for her inconsideration, so I don't have to settle for regular glazed half the time. Shit, just sell her a container of sprinkles for herself and the other porkers and save some for the rest of the customer base, for Christ's sake. It just makes economic sense."

"Uh… right," Shane mustered. "Are there any more left out front?"

Dean shrugged. "Don't know, but wouldn't count on it. I barely managed to grab this one before the rest of the animals out there got to the box."

He took another bite of the donut and wrinkled up his face. "Ugh. It's barely worth facing the day without sprinkles to greet me in the morning." He tossed the remainder unceremoniously into the small circular wastebasket by his desk. "I tell you, this world is going to hell in a handcart," he lectured, wiping sugary remnants from his hands. "But I suppose that's no surprise to you, Shane."

"No, sir," Shane replied, looking forlornly at the remains of the donut sitting atop crumpled balls of yellow paper in the trash, wondering if there was any way he could both retrieve it and maintain some fraction of his dignity. "In fact, that's sort of what I wanted to talk to you about."

"Oh?" Dean's eyebrows raised. "Hm. I assumed this was something to do with providing an excuse for your continued lateness. Or failing that, perhaps some strategy to move the beginning of your shifts back a half-hour so you'd somehow show up on the reports as early instead?"

Amused by his own joke, Dean grinned. Shane sweated, knowing the proper thing to do would be to laugh at Dean's jibe, but at the moment he couldn't find it in himself to do more than chuckle half-heartedly.

"Um, actually, the reason I was late today was that

something got messed up in my bank account and the gas got shut off at the house, so I wasn't able to get ready in time. I couldn't even get a decent shower this morning."

"Okay, sounds plausible," Dean allowed. "And last week?"

"L-last week?"

"Sure. You were late three out of five days last week as well, Shane. I presume you had hot water then, yes?"

"Well… yeah, but…"

"Exactly, Shane. So let's be honest: gas supply or no, on any given day we're looking at less-than-even odds you'll manage to stagger through those doors on time."

"I always stay over to make up any lateness, don't I?" Shane protested.

"Sure," Dean replied. "At least when I'm here late enough myself to make sure that happens. But that's not the point and you know it: the job starts at seven sharp, and that's when we need you here. Not five after, not seven ten, and definitely not seven twenty."

"All right, Dean. I promise I'll do better in the future," Shane said with a sigh. "But right now, the reason I came in here was that I needed to ask if I could possibly have an advance on my pay?"

"Ha, that's a good one." Dean held his stomach in mock amusement as Shane's face fell. "Oh, you weren't serious, were you? Because I seem to recall going out on a limb for you twice or thrice before, and those occasions didn't exactly work out in a manner I would call ideal."

"I'm getting those advances paid back, aren't I?"

"Sure, thanks to the twenty dollars a week I'm having withheld from each of your paychecks. And you're still three or four months out from being caught up. If I consent to any more advances, you'll owe us for each hour you work instead of the other way around."

"Come on, Dean, help me out here. I just need to get the gas turned back on so—"

"Let me stop you right there, Shane." Dean held up a hand. "I simply can't do any more to help you until you help yourself."

"Help… myself?"

"Sure. I mean, come on, guy: you have to give me something here. I have bosses too, and how do you think it looks to them when I have one employee who consistently fails to follow the rules time and again, and I not only can't get him in line but then I turn around and reward him with advance pay?" He shook his head. "I can't deny you're good on the phones when your head isn't in the clouds or up your own ass, Shane, but those times seem to get fewer and farther between every day. Honestly, the bottom line is that I like having you here, but I simply can't put myself out on a limb to cover for you anymore."

Shane bit his lip. "I get it."

"Do you? Do you really?" Dean came out from behind his desk and put his hand on Shane's shoulder paternally. The well-intentioned gesture stung coming from someone within a year of Shane's own age. "Because I hate to say it —really, I do—but we're coming to the end of the line here, the way things have been going."

"Yeah, I know," Shane mumbled. "I'm just… having a hard time lately, Dean."

Dean looked down. "I know, buddy. I know. But when we're here, I have to be your boss, not your friend. You can't make it my problem to sort out your problems. I have a full-time job of my own to protect and a wife to think of, and we're a long way from the band days. It's…" Dean looked away.

"What? It's what?"

"It's just that… well, honestly, I'm beginning to wonder

if I even did you any favor at all by bringing you on here, Shane." He sighed. "I'm starting to think maybe what you need is to learn to sink or swim on your own. Maybe then you'd be able to figure out how to make ends meet without coming to me every other paycheck."

Shane's eyes widened in panic. "Oh fuck, Dean, come on, man. I just need a couple more months and a little bit of luck to turn things around."

"So you say," Dean answered. "Seems to me I've heard that story a time or two already, though."

"That doesn't make it any less true. Look, I'm gradually getting the other advances paid back, and I'll make more of an effort to get here on time—really I will. But if I don't get the gas turned back on, that's going to be tough to pull off unless you want me coming in smelling like a homeless person."

"And what about your girlfriend?"

"Jewel? What about her?"

"She has a job, yeah? Why can't she be handling this problem while you're here at work?"

"This wasn't her fault, Dean. She contributes her share, I just… I just must've missed something in the budget this month."

Dean shook his head. "I bet you did." He stared out the window of his office; Shane followed his gaze, and they both watched in silence as a yellow finch landed on the bird feeder hanging from the tree outside, trilled its song, ate its fill, and flew away contentedly.

"Beautiful," Dean whispered to no one in particular before clearing his throat loudly and turning back to Shane. "Listen, Shane. Officially, as your supervisor, I'm at the end of my rope here. You get it? I can't do anything else to help you from behind this desk." He pointed at the paper-strewn surface beside them.

"I know, Dean. I get it."

"But… look," Dean said. "If you're really that deep in it, if it's really an emergency, if and only if every other avenue fails, I might—might!—be able to float you a short-term loan."

Shane brightened. "Really? Are you serious?"

"Don't get too excited yet," Dean said. "This would be strictly on a personal level, so for fuck's sake don't go telling anyone else here. And I'd have to run it by Marissa before I do anything—hell, I probably should have called her before even saying anything to you. But if that's what it's down to, I can't just stand by and let you be put out on the street either. So tell me straight: is that where you're at right now?"

Shane paused before answering. "Honestly? I don't think so. Not yet. I have a few more calls to make before I'm down to that."

"Not in the next few hours, I hope?"

"No, it can wait until lunch."

"It'll have to," Dean said. "Because as long as you're here, I need you on those phones with your head in the game. Can you do that?"

"I… sure. Yeah, of course."

"Good man." He clapped Shane on the back. "See? Step back, get a little perspective on your problems, and things don't seem as dark, do they?"

"I suppose not." Shane gritted his teeth as he exited Dean's office. All around, eyes turned away hurriedly, pretending to focus on their work. "Should I close the door behind me?"

"No, leave it open," Dean replied. "There's always the chance someone besides you might have a problem they need to bring before me."

"God forbid," Shane muttered under his breath just

quietly enough for his voice not to carry as he detoured into the kitchen on his way back towards his waiting cubicle.

At the sight of the big pink donut box sitting on the counter, 'Sidekick Artisan Doughnuts' emblazoned on its lid in huge, looping script lettering, his stomach rumbled, reminding him of that half-eaten glazed in Dean's trash.

Anxiously, he flipped it open, only to find it bare save for a few tantalizing smears of icing.

"Why would you leave an empty box out on the fucking counter, you goddamn savages," Shane asked quietly, scraping his finger through the leftover sugary glop before tossing the box into the trash. His stomach gurgled again, only teased by the scant sustenance of the icing remnants, and he rummaged furtively through the fridge and kitchen cabinets, hoping to find some leftovers he could scavenge without arousing the ire of the lunch-room police who diligently checked and double-checked every last named and labeled item.

After a search more thorough than many police investigations, all Shane managed to find was an ancient fortune cookie, stamped with a sell-by date more than eight months past. "Better than nothing," he told himself, tearing the package open and crushing the stiff cookie in one hand. After shoving the broken cookie pieces into his mouth, he found them slightly drier and more tasteless than usual, but otherwise more or less edible even if they failed to halt his stomach's rumbling.

Still, trudging to his desk he found himself disconcerted. It wasn't so much that he'd really been looking forward to whatever message the cookie had to give him, but finding it bereft of any fortune whatsoever was somehow more unsettling than he might have imagined.

A few hours later, Shane's head was pounding—both

from the relentless chatter of the customers he'd managed to counsel and the constant pressure of the stiff plastic earphones pushing against either side of his head. Generally, he enjoyed the aspects of the job that involved speaking with people, but as the workday progressed he found it increasingly difficult to concentrate on the substance of the callers' issues, each seemingly more trivial than the last.

A few had even dared to call him out on his lack of attentiveness after he'd failed to accurately parrot every detail of their complaints back to them, arrogantly demanding their calls be elevated to his supervisor or manager. Fortunately, the call center representative designated to play supervisor for that shift had not seemed to notice anything out of the ordinary—customers were always getting up in arms about one thing or another, most of which amounted to jack fucking squat—so Shane had luckily managed to dodge further additions to his disciplinary file.

One particularly irate caller even got bounced back to him after getting disconnected, yet showed not the slightest indication of realization that she was repeating her tale of personal affront to the same individual she held responsible for her not being able to remember her own password, and whose livelihood she'd previously threatened only a handful of minutes earlier.

By the time lunchtime rolled around, the last thing in the world Shane wanted to do was spend more time on the phone. But unfortunately circumstances dictated otherwise, so he shuffled back out to the employee parking lot, sat in his car, and dialed the number for the gas company's service line—already programmed into his phone from the last time he'd been forced to negotiate with them.

"Morgan County Gas Utility, this is Laura speaking," a

chipper voice chirped down the line at him. "How may I assist you today?"

"Good afternoon, Laura," Shane carefully enunciated, his habituated telephone manners kicking in automatically. "This is Shane Stone, Shane E. Stone. I'm a… customer of yours?" It sounded like a question, like the issue was in doubt.

"Yes, of course, Mister Stone," the cheerful voice replied. "What can I do for you?"

"Well, Laura, I hope you can help clear something up for me. When I got up this morning and hopped in my shower, I found that I didn't have any hot water, so I was wondering what happened there."

"I'm very sorry to hear that, sir. Could I have the name on the account, please?"

Shane sighed. "Shane, E as in elephant, Stone."

"Great. And can you verify the last four digits of your social security number?"

"Oh-nine-oh-two."

"Great, thanks, Mister Stone. I'm bringing up your account now."

The line dropped off into a distant hum as Laura silently reviewed the litany of previous offenses Shane imagined must be attached to his name in their system. How far back did it go, he wondered? If every call he'd ever had to make regarding his gas service was logged there, she could be reading for a while.

When she spoke again, Shane thought he detected a distinct change in her tone. "Here we are, Mister Stone. Yes, I'm afraid it looks like your gas service was shut off yesterday due to nonpayment. But if you have a credit card on hand, I can take care of that for you right now?"

"Well, Laura, the thing is that I'm a hundred percent

certain I sent the check in already, so this whole thing is a little bit confusing to me."

"Ah," she replied, and into that single syllable Shane heard any number of implied rebukes: possibly 'I just read your file, sir, how dumb do you think I am', or 'Don't try to scam me you degenerate scumbag, just pay your bills on time like everyone else in the world', or even 'I'm so glad my husband has a good job and isn't an irresponsible, lying piece of shit like you, Mister Stone'.

But Laura said only, "Well, I'm afraid it doesn't look like we ever received that check, sir."

"That's kind of what I figured. But I definitely sent it, so…" Shane left the sentence hanging, hoping Laura would jump in to fill in the blank to his benefit without further prompting.

"I'm afraid I can't authorize the account reactivation without receiving payment of some kind, sir."

Blinking, Shane wiped the sweat from his forehead, the hot sun reflecting directly into his eyes. "Sure, sure, I understand. But what I'm afraid of is that if I pay you now, and then the check gets there tomorrow or even later today, then, well… you see my problem?"

"We've already received our mail delivery for the day, sir," Laura declared flatly.

"Tomorrow, then. But then if I've paid you already, and that check gets applied to the account as well, then I'll have paid double the amount I actually owe."

"Any amount surplus to the amount owed would be applied to your next month's bill, sir."

"Yes, of course, but…" He trailed off, not wanting to admit how severely his budget would be overstrained by such an expenditure to the faceless voice on the line. "It's the principle of the thing."

"Sir," she said, a noticeably steelier tone evident in her

voice. "The system won't let me dispatch a technician to turn your gas back on without receiving payment of some sort. Are you sure you wouldn't rather—"

"I'll have to call you back," he blurted, interrupting her midsentence. "I just… I don't have my credit cards on me right at the moment."

Coolly, she answered, "I understand, sir," and he knew that she did. "Just be aware that after six p.m. this evening, no one will be on hand to verify payment until we reopen at seven a.m. tomorrow."

"Got it," he mumbled, already knowing their hours all too well. "Thanks for your help, Laura."

"No problem, sir," she replied, just as cheerful as at the outset of their conversation.

Damn it, he thought, gripping his phone so tightly his knuckles whitened. Damn it, damn it, damn it.

Out of the corner of his eye, he saw a group of co-workers laughing amongst themselves as they headed out to lunch, each no doubt about to spend upwards of ten dollars or more for one of the unhealthy, indulgent sodium-laden meals available at the many fast-food establishments in the area.

Turning his head away, hoping not to be spotted, his breathing already heavy with anxiety, he lifted his phone to his face, scrolled down his contact list to a number programmed with the first name DONOT and the last name ANSWER, then dialed it.

Four times, it rang.

Finally, the line opened.

"Yeah?" The voice on the other end of the line was gruff and curt, as if important business had been put on hold.

"I need to talk to Cole," Shane said.

"Sorry, pal, think you've got a wrong number. No one here by that name."

"Come on, Lukas," Shane shouted into the phone. "Just put me through to Cole, will you? I know he's there."

"Oh yeah? What makes you so sure?"

"When you picked up, I could hear him in the background saying to tell me he's not there."

"If you're so smart, then you should know the man really, really doesn't want to talk to you, Stone. Unless you're calling to set up repayment?"

"No, I..." Shane fell silent, struggling to complete his sentence.

"Yeah, that's what I thought. Look, bro, trust me. It's for your own protection. The man doesn't want to have to—"

"I don't have any choice. Please, Lukas, just tell him I'm at the end of my rope. I don't have anywhere else to turn."

He heard the mouthpiece of the phone on the other end of the line being covered, then there was nothing but silence for five seconds, then ten, then twenty.

A whiff of pollen drifted through Shane's open car window; his nose tickled as his allergies inflamed, and he stifled a rising cough.

Finally, a familiar dry, cracked voice came down the line: "Hello, Shane."

"Cole, thank god you agreed to talk to me."

"You may want to hold off on those thanks for a moment yet," the voice enunciated. "I gather you're not calling to tell me you have my money."

"No, but—"

"Shane, Shane, Shane. Do you have the slightest inkling how lucky you truly are? Anyone else in your position would be doing their level best to get me to forget about their existence entirely: staying out of public places, hiding their face from the light, and flinching every time they heard so much as a car backfiring. At the very least, I'd like to think they'd have the common sense and decency not to rub my face in my past indiscretions—and possibly flawed judgment—in entrusting unworthy individuals with my precious, limited resources. Yet here you are, not only not staying out of my way, but insisting upon forcing a confrontation I was all too willing to put off, making personal demands upon my even more precariously limited time. I'll tell you frankly, it's enough to make one question his sanity—or at least yours."

"I know, Cole, and I'm sorry. And I know how much I owe you already, but I don't have anywhere else to turn. My gas got shut off this morning and—"

"Stop right there," Cole interrupted. "That is not the problem. Or rather, it's not my problem, and I must admit I'm finding it exceedingly difficult to empathize with your personal issues at the present moment.

"No, Shane," he continued, "in my view the true problem is that your actions have consequences in this world. You see, whether you are aware of it or not, the example you set is looked to by others. And when said consequences fail to match up to expectations, individuals who find themselves in positions similar to yours may quite reasonably expect their actions to elicit similar results. You see my dilemma?"

"It wasn't my fault, Cole. You know it wasn't my fault."

"I know nothing of the sort," Cole said.

"Come on," Shane pleaded. "I used to help you out back in the day."

"Yes, Shane, you did," Cole said. "And that's the only reason you're still walking around in broad daylight with four fully functioning limbs. But that was a long time ago, now. And whatever happened back in the day, that doesn't get me my money back, does it now?"

"I promised I'd pay you back the second I could, didn't I?"

"You did," Cole said. "But the more time passes, the less my acceptance of that promise strikes me as a wise decision. And speaking quite frankly, this call seems like yet more confirmation of my suspicions."

"You'll get your money, Cole. I swear you'll get your money."

"Oh, I know I will. That fact was never in question. The only issue remaining to be resolved is just how much effort you're going to make me go to in order to obtain that repayment? Speaking as a busy man, I'd much prefer it be less, of course, but sometimes what must be done is what must be done."

"What… what do you mean? What must be done?"

"Oh, nothing in particular," Cole said. "I'm just speaking generally, regarding maxims I've found accurate more often than not. Almost axiomatic, really. You understand."

Shane wasn't sure he did. But the implication of Cole's enigmatic words couldn't mean anything good for him.

"But apropos of nothing in particular," Cole continued, "how's that girlfriend of yours—Jewel, isn't it? Still waiting tables at Sparky's?"

Shane's tongue went bone dry. "Jewel, yes. She… she's still at Sparky's, but she's bartending now."

"Bartending," Cole repeated. "Better money, worse hours, if I remember correctly from my days dating bar wenches and waitresses. Has that been your experience?"

"Uh… I suppose so."

"Mm. Tough to keep a relationship like that together

over the long haul, I'd imagine. At least when you don't work the same hours. Then again, you may not have to worry about that much longer."

"What's that supposed to mean?" Sweat dripped from Shane's armpits; his shirt already damp.

"Hm? Oh, nothing, nothing at all. Just thinking out loud about the long-term impact of ill-advised financial decisions on the health of one's romantic life. You know how it goes. Some types of women like to be taken care of more than others, that's all I'm saying. Some need that kind of treatment, and they'll go where they can find it."

Shane's mind raced, his palms sweating, his throat closing up. "Y-yeah," he stammered. "I think I need to go now. Anyway, sorry for disturbing you, Cole."

"Of course, Shane. Think nothing of it. Well, actually, do think something of it. I wish I could say it was nice speaking with you this afternoon, but you know how I dislike unnecessary falsehoods. So instead, let's simply conclude this conversation with my fervent hope that on the next occasion we speak, you will have better news for me. Can you promise me that?"

"I…" Shane smacked his dry lips, his mouth a desert. "I'll try, Cole."

"I suppose that's the best I can hope for at the moment. Good day to you, Shane."

The line went dead.

Barely caring if anyone was around to see him, Shane collapsed forward onto his steering wheel, sweat dripping down his neck, clammy palms clutched around his phone.

"Fuck," he muttered. "Fuck, fuck, fuck."

After taking several deep breaths, attempting to steady himself, Shane stared off into the distance for a full minute, maybe more. In the trees above Shane's Aspire, the birds chirped, carefree and cheerful; the wind blew through his car interior, raising goosebumps on his skin as the dampness saturating his shirt slowly evaporated. Pulled by the breeze, the thick, salty fried-beef smell emitted by the fast-food burger joint across the road's exhaust fan drifted lazily into his nostrils, reminding him once more of his empty stomach and the minutes ticking away on his rapidly diminishing lunch break.

Eventually, he raised his phone to his eyes. With reluctance, he opened his contacts and scrolled down the list, each name a vivid reminder of some past mistake, humiliation, or disaster.

Of the few individuals he was still on speaking terms with, their ironclad disinclinations to lend him money in the past were likely all that had kept him from falling from their grace to date.

Of those he wasn't, none leaped out at him as likely to rescind their quite reasonable and entirely valid decisions.

But he had to try.

He dialed a number, half-expecting to find it changed, a jolt of nerves shooting down his spine at the sound of ringing.

His breath caught in his throat as the line opened and he heard a familiar, dusty ambience, followed by a few clipped, tense syllables in a slightly hoarse female voice: "Hello, Shane."

"Uh… hi," he said, his voice barely above a whisper. "Listen… I know I said I wouldn't call, but this is an emergency and I don't have anywhere else to turn."

There was a sigh of deeply ingrained weariness. "An emergency." It was not a question.

"Yeah. It… it's too much to go into the whole thing right now, but basically, our gas was shut off this morning, and the other utilities won't be far behind. I just need enough to get caught up, and then after that, I swear, I should be able to start getting everything paid back."

"Our?"

"Er… yeah. Mine and Jewel's."

"Ah. You're still with that woman, then. Well, I suppose I owe your father ten dollars then."

"Ten dollars?"

"Yes. My thinking was that you'd have brains enough not to move in with someone like that, but your father said otherwise. Oh, how was it that he put it? Something like, 'No matter how bad she is for him, that boy would follow whatever woman gives him the time of day until the sun burns out in the sky.' Only the language he used was a bit more colorful than I'm willing to repeat on the phone."

Shane's cheeks flushed hot and red. "Don't talk about her that way. You don't even know her."

"Hmph," she said. "And yet, here you are calling for yet more money. It seems I know all I need to know."

"That just goes to show how wrong you are, Kathleen. She had nothing to do with this, it was all my fuck up."

"Oh, I have no doubt about that, Shane. But if she was really the type of woman you need to be with, by now she'd have shaped you into the more responsible person we've always known you could be. Instead, you continue on in the same tiresome paths you've been treading for far too long, despite showing no signs whatsoever of ever getting ahead. Don't you ever get tired of being wrong? Aren't you tired of this by now? I know I am. I'm absolutely certain your father is. Really, Shane: is it worth all this struggle and frustration just to prove some ridiculous point?"

"I'm not trying to prove a point, Mom."

"Oh, now it's 'Mom', is it? How endearing. What

happened to 'Kathleen'? Trying to ingratiate yourself with my few remaining maternal instincts, I suppose?"

"I just…" Shane sighed, defeated. "You know what, never mind. I should have known I was wasting my time calling here."

"Yes, you really should have. I trust you won't make that mistake again anytime soon."

The line closed without further formality.

Shane glared at the phone gripped tightly in his palm, the veins in the backs of his fingers popping out. He wanted to throw it in frustration, but he held back, knowing he didn't have even a fraction of the money it would take to repair or replace it.

God damn it, he thought. And now I don't even have enough time left to go through a drive-through before my break is done. His stomach rumbled in sympathy with his thoughts, as if confirming its state of emptiness.

"Screw it," he said, turning his ignition over and peeling out of the parking lot in a cloud of dust. If Dean didn't let him go this morning, he wasn't going to fire him over taking an extra ten to grab a sandwich. Right?

CHAPTER TWO

"Fuck this stupid day," Shane mumbled to himself, slumped on the uncomfortable bus bench with his head in his hands.

As the seven-ten westbound city bus finally approached, only twelve minutes late, he glared over at his Aspire sitting inert at the far edge of the parking lot where he'd just barely managed to push it, grunting and groaning all the way, after it died midway through the return trip from the sandwich shop.

Of course, it wasn't until the second he finally shoved it into place that a carload of his co-workers came wheeling into the lot, mouths full of questions about what had happened to it and lies about how happy they would have been to help him push it to safety, if only they'd been there. Shane half-suspected they'd spotted him straining and sweating along the side of the road and held back until the moment they could come swooping in with their false sympathies for his plight—none of them were offering him money out of their pockets to bail him out, were they? So fuck them all.

Shane hadn't bothered to call a mechanic, either after breaking down or shoving the car back to the lot. Whether it was the alternator again or some other, more arcane issue preventing the car from running properly, getting it fixed came no higher than third or fourth in the list of problems requiring immediate attention and funding he didn't have.

At least Dean had been understanding at the lateness of his return, merely shaking his head with amusement at the absurdity of it all. "Only you," he'd said, and Shane had to agree.

Shane wasn't sure why he always seemed to get the shit end of the stick where luck was concerned, but at least Dean was willing to let him stay extra late to cover both his morning and afternoon tardinesses, as well as to allow him an extra five minutes to wolf down the cold remains of the corned beef on rye he'd been driving back with when the Aspire died before making him jump back on the phones.

The problem with staying extra late, Shane had only realized afterwards, was that no one remained from whom he might have grabbed a ride. The second-shift operators had all been settled into their seats for well over an hour by the time Shane clocked out, by which time all of his usual co-workers had long since vacated the premises, Dean included.

At least Dean had checked in with him to see if he was doing all right before taking off for the day, even if he suspected Dean's repeated mention of having to run his loan offer by his wife was his way of saying that it probably wouldn't happen. In any case, it was the wrong kind of loan Dean was offering: the kind that would eventually have to be repaid. But Shane hadn't managed to uncover any more promising potential solutions over the past few hours, so any faint thread of hope was better than none.

Past six o'clock, bus service became far less frequent than during the day, so it was an extra twenty-two minutes after finally leaving work before a bus heading the right direction was scheduled to appear—and it was thirteen more past that before it finally rattled to a halt by the bus stop, its doors hissing open unwelcomingly. At least the bus stop was sheltered, keeping the rain that had started up around six-thirty from soaking him through, even if the blowing wind managed to wet his pant legs pretty good.

Shane pulled himself to his feet with an audible groan, feeling the weight of his body pulling him back down to earth. At least the long delay before the bus arrived had given him time to grab a hot chocolate and a bag of salt and vinegar chips to tide him over for the wait and fortify him for the ride, leaving him with just enough change to cover the two dollar-fifty cent fare.

Dropping the crumpled paper cup and chip bag into the bus stop trash can, he mounted the grimy black rubber-covered steps into the bus interior, pulling his hand from his pocket and sliding the quarters one by one into the farebox, each making an audible plink as they settled into place.

After the tenth quarter, he took a step past the white line demarcating the beginning of the bus aisle, only to be caught up short by the driver blocking his way with one meaty arm while shaking his head.

"Uh-uh, man," the driver grunted from behind thick glasses. He pointed to a sticker, freshly mounted to the side of the farebox: "Two seventy-five."

"Oh, for—" Shane rummaged through his pockets, already knowing what he'd find. "Look, all I've got is a five."

Wordlessly, the driver merely pointed at another sign reading NO CHANGE PROVIDED in red capital letters.

Shane glanced around at his fellow passengers in desperation; not one would even meet his eyes.

"Fine," Shane fumed, sliding the folded five-dollar bill into the farebox slot.

The driver withdrew his arm, allowing Shane to pass. "Thanks for choosing to ride with us today, sir."

"Don't mention it," Shane muttered as he lurched down the aisle, finding a seat three-quarters of the way back in front of a twentysomething college student staring at her phone with a book-stuffed backpack beside her and Hello Kitty headphones clamped firmly over her ears, behind a hunched-over white-haired woman who had to be eighty if she was a day. Neither the student fare nor the senior fare had risen even a cent, Shane had noticed.

He wondered whether the extra surplus from his fare would go to the bus system's coffers or the driver's pocket, unable to decide which eventuality would be more suiting to his predicament. The bus system, most likely—the driver was probably just another trapped soul like himself, shuffling from moment to moment, day to day in a seemingly endless struggle for mere survival. He didn't make the rules, after all.

Then again, maybe the driver was one of those guys who had it all figured out. Even if the take-home pay wasn't that great, he'd heard bus drivers got great benefits, and the job security was rock-solid thanks to the transit workers' union. Still, they had to go ten hours without so much as taking a leak; Shane shuddered at the prospect of enduring a shift without the option of ducking out to the can and staring at his phone for ten minutes or so whenever he felt overwhelmed.

He leaned his forehead against the cool glass of the bus

window, trying not to think about how long it had probably been since it had been cleaned as lights whizzed by
outside. He closed his eyes, relishing the muted
psychedelic display of red, white, and yellow lights
against his eyelids, his ears filled with the whir of the bus's
diesel engine and the muffled hip-hop coming from the
headphones of the passenger in the seat behind.

All went black as the bus went into the tunnel beneath
the Fourth Street bridge, and Shane sighed, savoring the
moment of peace while he had the opportunity. The
second he got home, Jewel would be on him, peppering
him with questions about why he hadn't managed to get
the hot water on and blaming him for the fact that she'd
have to go into work unshowered and unkempt, which
would likely lead to a decrease in her tip revenue, which
would likely lead to another confrontation he could do
nothing about. But just for a moment in the refuge of the
tunnel, he could drive his troubles from his mind and
simply float for a minute, pretending everything would be
all right in the end, somehow.

A piercing scream was immediately followed by a sick-
ening thud; the bus jolted to an abrupt stop, jolting Shane
into the back of the seat in front of his, then to the filthy
floor beneath.

"What the hell?" He rubbed his head ruefully,
wondering not for the first time why public buses didn't
have seat belts. Glancing around, his fellow passengers
seemed similarly befuddled; evidently such occurrences
were not a regular feature of the westbound line.

Intending to demand an explanation from the driver,
Shane began to rise from his seat, only to see the driver
bolt from the vehicle in a flash.

His eyes briefly met those of the headphone-wearing
passenger in the back of the bus; the girl shrugged and

turned back to her phone before Shane had a chance to say anything, and one by one, the remaining passengers followed suit. Only the senior citizen in the seat before him continued to crane her neck, her curiosity unsatisfied.

Shane was beginning to wonder whether anyone was going to tell them anything when, through the window, he spotted the driver pacing up and down at the side of the bus talking agitatedly into his phone. He couldn't make out any words over the idle rumble of the bus engine, but the sight of the civil servant's formerly passive, bored visage now distorted into a mask of frenzied panic filled him with anxious dread.

Two minutes went by, then three, then ten. Finally, the driver remounted the steps of the bus, coughing to clear his throat as one by one, each face turned in his direction.

"Ladies and gentlemen," the driver said, and somehow the overly formal style of the announcement chilled Shane's blood, underscoring the seriousness of the situation even more than anything else that had occurred thus far. "I'm afraid I'm forced to announce that we have reached the end of the line for our travels today. Please gather your belongings and exit the bus in an orderly fashion."

The eighty-year-old woman was the first to articulate the question at the front of every passenger's mind: "What happened?"

"It… somebody jumped off the top of the overpass as we were coming out of the tunnel," the driver said.

The girl in headphones put her hands to her mouth in shock. "Ohmigod. You mean he killed himself?"

"We don't know that for sure," said the driver. "But it looks that way."

An older man sitting with his back to the front of the bus shook his head knowingly. "Ain't nothing says it had to be a suicide. I hear the mafia throws scumbags who don't pay them back off of bridges all the time. Lot easier to let the traffic get rid of the evidence for you than bothering to do it yourself."

Shane's stomach turned.

"Regardless, the police have taken the matter out of our hands," the driver continued.

"What about another bus? Is anyone else coming to pick us up?" The older woman wasn't letting the driver off the hook that easily.

"No, I'm afraid the street will be closed for the indefinite future pending further investigation."

She pressed on: "What does that mean? What are we supposed to do?"

"That means this bus isn't moving an inch and no one is getting through here while the police try to figure this out," the driver said. "My best suggestion? Call a rideshare or taxicab from a few blocks away—that's what I'm going to do, after I give my statement to the cops. Otherwise, I guess you're walking."

The bus interior exploded into a commotion of voices attempting to remonstrate with the driver, demanding refunds or bus passes in reimbursement and exchanging offers to share hired vehicles and split the fares. Shane briefly considered adding his voice to theirs, but the lack of success the old lady faced in her attempt to extract any form of refund told him his efforts would likely meet no better outcome than his hope of getting change for his five earlier. Besides, it was obvious that the driver was singularly focused on getting everyone off the bus as quickly as possible so he could shut it down and get home himself. And no matter how many other passengers were headed in his direction, Shane didn't have any money to spare on a rideshare or taxi. No sense wasting any more time waiting for the rain to stop or for some better option to make itself known.

Shane stepped from the bus's side door, a groan emerging from deep in his lungs as his feet touched the ground and the doors hissed shut behind him, muting the din of the clamoring passengers on the bus. Immediately, raindrops speckled his face, and he pulled his light jacket tight around himself, resigned himself to a long, unpleasant trudge homeward.

He resisted the temptation to peek around the side of the bus at the carnage that had halted their forward progress; the whine of approaching sirens reminding him that while one person's troubles might be finished, the rest of the world continued onward apace, unmindful and uncaring.

Besides, he reminded himself, some things couldn't be unseen, and he suspected he would sleep better that night without the sight of whatever remained of the poor soul who had ended his days beneath the wheels of that bus rattling around in his brain. It was already bad enough that he couldn't get his speculations about what had led the man over that ledge out of his mind.

Walking home while cold rain beat down on one's head was never ideal, and while it was admittedly a stretch to think of any upside to his forced detour, it did at least provide him with more time to think. Granted, Shane had never been much of one to look on the bright side of life, as he'd always found relentlessly positive individuals mostly draining and deluded, but occasionally it seemed the only choices remaining to an individual in this life were to laugh or go irretrievably insane. Either way, none of the thoughts resulting from Shane's wet trudge homeward managed to illuminate any previously undiscovered escape routes from the bind in which Shane found himself, though he hardly expected them to.

Uncomfortable as he was, Shane was perfectly content to walk in silence, his face contorted in self-hate as he plodded onward placing one wet foot in front of another, not even bothering to stick his thumb out in hopes of catching a free ride. He didn't dare to hope for an easy way out to drop in his lap; the way his day had gone, any further surprises were almost certain to be unpleasant at best, and he decided to count it as a win if he somehow managed to get home without incurring major injury—far from a sure bet, given the way car after car shrieked by him, seemingly taking little account of either the slickness of the road or the beaten-down man trudging along the unpaved ruts at its side.

There was, at least, one small benefit to the late hour of his arrival: Jewel would long since have had to leave for work. Sure, she'd certainly be boiling with anger at him for failing to sort out the gas bill in time for her to bathe beforehand, but at least he could forestall that inevitable confrontation until after he'd had a quiet, relaxing evening to himself to decompress from the relentless train of shit he'd been forced to endure practically from the moment his eyes had opened.

Okay, so he wouldn't be able to take a hot shower to wash away the chill that had set into his bones two minutes into his homeward hike. It was still home, and the spring weather was sufficiently warm that neither of them would have to worry about freezing to death during the night. After he stripped off his sodden outfit, wrapped himself in some clean, comfortable clothes, popped open a beer and sparked up a bowl he'd be feeling almost human again. And once he'd gained the benefit of perspective as well as a much-needed break from the world dumping every problem it contained directly onto his head, perhaps he'd be able to figure out the exact best way of phrasing their predicament in such a way that he'd be able to avoid suffering the wrath of Jewel's ire. Most likely not, of course, but even the thought was enough to rekindle hope in Shane's heart.

That small ember of hope sputtered, flickered, and died the moment Shane turned the corner onto their street and saw Jewel's rickety moss-green Nissan Cube with the long scar down its left side parked in front of the house, exactly where it had been when he'd left that morning.

"Of course," Shane said aloud, unable to feel surprise at seeing the prospect of a much-needed evening of relaxation evaporate before his eyes. If anything, he berated himself for daring to get his hopes up—he should have known the world wouldn't allow him such an indulgence. Not that day.

Rain poured from the downspout, flooding the small patch of brown-and-green grass that passed for their front yard. At least the slapdash shingling job the landlord had done on the roof seemed to be holding up against the downpour for the moment, though if the wind kicked up much more Shane knew he'd probably find stray shingles scattered through the yard and street in the morning.

Shane leaped unsuccessfully across the accumulated pond that was their front walk, landing with a squelch that engulfed his already-chilled feet up to his ankles and sent a sheaf of water splashing against the house's worn brown vinyl siding, originally manufactured to mimic the appearance of cypress wood but now so bleached by the sun that its dingy patina resembled nothing so much as old rubber doorstops.

Finally standing before the front door, water dripping from his eyebrows down his cheeks, Shane shivered.

Breathing deeply, he braced himself, his shoulders tensing as he grasped the front doorknob and turned.

The second the door cracked open, a barrage of high-energy dance music blared out at him, shortly followed by a thick cloud of marijuana smoke, and Shane sighed deeply.

Inside, Jewel sat slumped on the couch, long black hair tied back in a sloppy ponytail, a glass of red wine in one hand and a joint in the other. Her trim body was clad in well-worn workout clothes, though she displayed no signs of having recently exercised: her armpits were free of sweat, the four-dollar bottle of cabernet sauvignon on the coffee table before her was nearly empty, and the joint was nearly burned down to nothing.

Shane stepped across the threshold and pulled his saturated shoes from his feet, setting them by the door with a wet thump.

Jewel glanced up at him, apparently just now alerted to his presence. She set her glass down to reach for her phone and shut the music off.

"Well, well, look who finally decided to show his face," she slurred, the tone of her voice making Shane speculate whether she was working on her first or second bottle of wine. "I was starting to wonder if you'd decided to find us someplace else to sleep tonight without bothering to tell me beforehand. I almost wouldn't mind if it was someplace with hot water."

"No, I, uh… my car broke down at lunch, and I couldn't get it fixed." He decided Jewel was likely in little mood to hear the gruesome details of his workday.

"Couldn't get the gas taken care of either, huh?"

"No, sorry. I was hoping—"

"I was hoping too," she cut him off. "Hoping to take a

fucking shower sometime today. But that doesn't look like it's going to happen either, is it?"

"I called, honey, but they wouldn't listen to me. Weren't you supposed to be working tonight?" He doubted she'd let him get away with it for long, but changing the conversation to the subject of Jewel's workplace was generally a surefire diversion, if a temporary one.

Her face screwed up in irritation. "Oh, those assholes called me ten minutes before I was supposed to leave and said business was slow, the fuckers."

"Well, it is raining out."

"So fucking what? Half the time, rain means more business, not less. I bet that bitch Loretta put the idea in the boss's head that I've been stealing or some shit, and this is their way of rooting me out. Like I'd be sitting here smelling like last night's late rush if I'd really been ripping them off, dumb pieces of shit."

"Did you tell them that?"

"Of course not. What would be the point? They'll find what they want to find. Those girls all hate me. If they want to find evidence to get rid of me, they'll do it one way or another."

Unspoken was the certainty that Jewel had been too embarrassed to tell anyone that her hot water had been shut off, that her boyfriend was unable to keep the bills paid, and that she would have had to go in to work unshowered. Shane wondered how much of what he was being told would be verified by her co-workers or manager, were he to have the inclination to call and check.

"Well, don't worry about it too much, baby," Shane said. "We'll muddle through somehow. We always do."

"Easy for you to say," she shot back.

"Ugh," Shane said. "None of this is any easier for me than it is for you, baby."

"Isn't it? Sometimes I wonder," she muttered, emptied the dregs of the cabernet into her glass, gulped it down, finished the last puffs of the joint, ashed the roach out in the cannabis leaf-shaped tray on the coffee table, and stared down at the floor in silence.

Shane groaned, put his hand to his forehead, shut his eyes and tilted his head back until the glare of the overhead light shone through his eyelids.

In that second, Shane had one of those instantaneous moments of clarity one sometimes has during any relationship, where in the space of a microsecond you re-experience every moment that brought you to that point in time, see the ramifications of every action you've ever taken in relation to that other person, and understand how every decision both of you made during that timeframe brought you inexorably to that point—but also, you simultaneously understand that no matter what, things could never have been any other way.

And in that moment, somehow you know that what you do next could determine the entire course of the rest of your life, one way or another, and the bitch of it was you would never know whether it was ultimately for the better or for worse.

In that moment, Shane saw everything that had brought him and Jewel closer together and everything that kept them apart, and he knew without even a sliver of doubt that she was at the center of every choice he'd made. Because standing there in their tiny living room, looking down at her on their beaten-down couch hanging her head as low as he'd ever seen it, he was forced to finally admit to himself what he'd resisted for so long: he couldn't live without her, because she was his heart.

She might not feel the same way about him, not exactly, and that was okay—he didn't need her to. But for Shane, she was utterly intrinsic to the construction of his life, and she had been ever since that first second after he'd seen her and realized how screwed he was, because from that point forward he was no longer making decisions based on what was best for himself—the only smart decisions, as his mother and father had hammered into his head ad nauseam over the course of his childhood.

No, from then on, whether he realized it at the time or not, every choice had been made on the basis of whether it was right for her, for them, for their future. And he couldn't deny that had he made those same choices with only himself at heart—the way he'd made every choice in every relationship he'd ever been in before meeting Jewel—he'd have been better off at that point in time, at least financially.

But—and this was the real fuckery of the situation—because he wouldn't have had Jewel there with him, it would have been meaningless. Totally, utterly meaningless and empty. Like his life before he met her, like his life would be if he managed to lose her.

Even now, with the sight of her piss drunk filling his eyes and mind, her lip twisted in resentment and blame, teetering on the edge of one of her horrible toxic fits of anger in which she blamed him for everything wrong in her life, including problems reaching back a decade or two before they had even met, he loved her purely and without reservation. And he knew without a doubt that if Jewel were to exit his life, he might continue to live on, but only as a heartless husk of a man without point to his existence. If Shane had a future at all—and he wasn't at all certain that he did, not even a shitty one—it was with Jewel. And really, he had never had any choice in the matter.

In the days to come, this moment of clarity would frequently come back to Shane in instants of quietude—rays of artificial light penetrating his lids, everything orange as life swirled around him, Jewel on the couch before and below him, oblivious to the turmoil in his head. Eventually, he would come to recognize it as one of the few true peak experiences of his life, when he was the most himself he would ever be, when he might have changed everything—but he would also recognize that to have done so, everything would have had to be different anyway, so in truth he had never had even a hope of a prayer of changing either of their courses, even if he'd wanted to. Yet he would always revel in the memory of that moment and know that, God willing, if he was granted time to reflect back over his life at its end, that singular moment of clarity would be featured prominently, whether flashing before his eyes on his deathbed or in a sudden rush as his consciousness ebbed from that plane.

Shane saw his actions then as though from outside his body, and he wondered if he was capable of doing other than what had been foreordained, knowing as he asked that the answer was, and always had been, 'no.'

He saw his hand reach for his pocket, extract his phone, and open up the bank app; he saw himself place his thumb on the home button to unlock the account and shove the display in front of Jewel's face.

"There, see for yourself," he heard his own voice sputter. "What the fuck am I supposed to do with that?"

Jewel's eyes widened, more than he'd ever seen. For a few seconds she actually seemed to be struck speechless—a state he could not remember having afflicted her ever before, not even once.

Eventually, she took the phone from his hand and stared at it a few moments more. She touched its surface, clicking around intently, seemingly oblivious to her boyfriend standing over her, expectantly awaiting a reply. It was infuriating how calm she suddenly was, as if it was a given that Shane would stand there forever waiting for her to finish whatever the hell she thought she was doing.

After the passage of an eon or more, she handed the phone back to him. Finally, she said, "I guess that's the question, isn't it?"

Jewel patted the sofa cushion beside her. "Here, sit down while I grab another wine glass. I assume you want some?"

"Uh, sure," Shane muttered, rubbing his head as she disappeared into the kitchen.

He sat on the sofa where her hand had indicated, and only then did he look at his phone. There, on the screen, he saw what she had seen: CURRENT BALANCE: $41,512.57.

He blinked, looked away, looked back. It was still there.

There was a soft pop and Jewel reentered the room, an empty wine glass in one hand, a freshly opened four-dollar bottle of shiraz in the other.

He took the glass, holding it up as she filled it nearly to the brim, did the same with her own glass, then sat beside him.

She took a sip and turned to him. "You know we have to be smart about this, Shane," she said. "It's a damn good thing you brought this to me before you did anything crazy or stupid, like surprise me with an expensive present or rent a ritzy hotel suite or anything like that."

He swallowed a third of his glass in one gulp. "You think I'm stupid? Or crazy?"

Jewel shook her head. "No, that's not what I'm trying to say. But money has a way of making people act crazy and stupid."

Shane looked back at his phone, turned off the screen and set it on the coffee table between them, next to the two-thirds empty bottle of shiraz. "Yeah, okay."

She put her hand on his arm. "Don't you see? This is our chance. But we only have one shot at this, and that's why we have to be smart."

"Okay," he said again. "Yeah. You're right." It was striking how sober she suddenly appeared, as well as how quick she was to treat the money as belonging to both of them, despite the fact that it was in his account. He pondered briefly how things might be different if the shoe were on the other foot, then shook his head, not anxious to tug too firmly on that particular thread.

"Of course," he added, "this is all assuming the money is still there in the morning when we wake up."

"Sure, sure," she agreed, gesturing at the room around them. "And this house could collapse tonight, or a meteor could drop out of the sky and kill us both. But we can't plan for every possible eventuality, and we can't control whether or not that money actually stays there long enough for us to do anything with it."

"All right, all right," he said. "So assuming it stays there and we don't immediately get a notice that the bank is reclaiming it, how should we proceed from this point?"

Jewel placed her thumb and finger to her lips in thought. "Well, first of all, do you have any idea at all how this could have happened?"

"Not a clue," Shane answered. "There weren't any scheduled transfers coming in, I don't get paid for another week and a half. And I certainly wasn't expecting anything on that scale, like, ever."

He paused for a moment before continuing. "But, thinking about it, to be totally honest, I barely understand how they manage to keep any of that shit straight anyway.

I mean, companies and people are constantly transferring money all over the place, all the time, every moment of every day, right? Not to mention all this cryptocurrency, bitcoin and shit. Dollars to doughnuts someone just typed in an account number wrong, just got it off by one digit and it ended up in my account. And maybe as soon as they realize what they did, they're going to want that money back, to send it on to whoever was supposed to get it in the first place."

"Maybe, maybe," Jewel mused. "And maybe not. Think, Shane: is there, the slightest chance, any remote possibility this might even be, you know, legit? Like, I don't know, a tax refund? Or an inheritance from some relative you didn't even know died?"

He shook his head, now wondering how much Jewel had picked up about his family's finances. "Not a chance. My family has made it very clear I'm not to expect anything there, either now or later. And I'm still in the hole to the government for last year's taxes."

And the year before, he added silently to himself.

"Okay," she said, tapping her lips repeatedly. "So let's say the money isn't legitimately ours, but that it also isn't discovered for at least a couple of weeks. Where does that leave us?"

She stopped and looked up at the ceiling for a moment. "I mean, let's be real," she continued. "Sure, forty-one grand is more money than either one of us could reason- ably have expected to put together any time soon, but it's not really that much money. Sure, it's enough for a car or two, and enough that someone is most likely going to notice it missing sooner or later, but it isn't, like, a million or anything either."

"No, it isn't," Shane agreed. "But it is well over ten grand. So that means the bank has to report it, so chances are more than even that someone somewhere is bound to realize things aren't adding up eventually, like when they run payroll or do their monthly books or whatever. They have to. "

"Yeah," Jewel said. "They will, sooner or later." She rubbed her chin and took another sip. "So we don't know how long we have. But we have the run of this money for however long that is. If we can use it somehow in that time to, you know, multiply it, whatever we make by the time they come back asking for it would be ours to keep, free and clear."

He squinted at her. "I hope you're not thinking of gambling with it?"

She shook her head vigorously. "Fuck no. That shit is for suckers. Anyone who can do basic math should know the house is the only real winner there. And we probably don't have anything close to the kind of time it would take for either of us to become professional-level poker players."

Shane nodded in agreement; he'd never managed to come out ahead even just playing Texas hold-em with friends. And even though Jewel was a lot better than he was at playing her cards close to the vest in general, at least in the proverbial sense, she had never shown so much as the slightest interest in the game.

"So what are our options, then?" he asked. "Neither of us know nearly enough about the stock market or other legitimate investments to be able to dance around all those regulations, especially with 'borrowed' money, even if we knew what the fuck to do with it."

"No, we can't do that either," she agreed. "We need something a fuck of a lot more certain if we're going to come out of this thing on top."

"So let's boil it down. What we need is an almost

certain way of making a lot of money, and quickly, with virtually no risk. Easy peasy," he said, voice crackling with sarcasm.

Jewel grimaced. "Well, not with that attitude. Come on, let's figure out exactly what we're really working with here."

After extracting a pen from the bowels of her purse, she reached under the coffee table, grabbed a stray advertising flyer for a local pizza delivery service, flipped it over, and drew a line down the center of the paper. At the top of the left column, she wrote '41,500'.

"All right," she said. "Let's assume we don't try to multiply the money, but instead use it to pay down our various debts. Here are our assets, which at this point include next to nothing besides what we have here." In the right-hand column, she began scribbling numbers: "And here's what we owe for gas, water, and electric… this is roughly what we still owe on the cars… here's rent, including this month and the amount we're behind… here's how much we have piled up on the various credit cards… and here's the balance of my student loan. We spend about this much on food, keeping the cars running, and other household incidentals each month, and about this much on drinks, weed, and other… let's call them 'entertainment-related' expenses. Is that it? Oh, wait," she swiftly corrected herself. "Can't forget the taxman, like you said. And we'll need to finally get some health insurance, now that we have the leeway to do so."

Wincing, Shane peered at the paper as Jewel wrote. The numbers were adding up quickly, and Jewel didn't even have their single largest expense listed. Not her fault, of course; she'd had to have known about it first.

She opened her phone's calculator app, did some quick calculations, and wrote the total at the bottom. The figure was disappointingly small; Shane could almost feel the wind leaving his sails.

"Well," she said. "Not enough for us to live high on the hog. Not for very long, at least. But if we're smart about it, we should be able to buy ourselves some breathing room, if not much else. Thank fuck neither of us has any kids to support or alimony to pay."

Shane coughed. "I'm, uh… I'm also about fifteen hundred dollars away from being paid up on those advances from work."

She wrinkled her nose, adding the figure to the list. "Oh yeah. I forgot about that. Plus, we'll definitely need to drop at least two or three thousand to either get the cars fixed up to the point where they'll quit breaking down every couple of weeks or to replace them with more reliable transportation. Still, not too bad, all things considered."

He took a deep breath. "That's not all, honey."

Jewel frowned at him. "What do you mean, that's not all? What am I leaving out?"

He looked away from her eyes. "I mean, I have another outstanding debt. One I didn't tell you about, because, well… it's my problem and mine alone. I didn't want you to have to worry about it."

She shook her head. "That's not how these things work, Shane. Just tell me. What is it?"

"No, really, honey—this goes back to before you and I ever got together in the first place. It was nothing to do with you."

"Just spit it out and stop with the excuses," she said, her jaw tightening. "The longer you hold me in suspense, the madder I'm going to be."

"Look," he sputtered. "I have it under control. If Cole

was going to do anything about it, he would have done so years ago."

Her eyes went wide and her jaw dropped open. "Cole? Cole Waters? You owe money to Cole Waters?" She put her head in her hands. "Oh, fuck, Shane. That guy kills people. Or has them killed. Either way, people end up dead for crossing him."

"I know how it sounds, honey. But really—Cole and I go way back. And most of that stuff people say about him is just talk, to keep people on their toes, keep them guessing."

She looked askew at him. "So you say."

"I'm still here, aren't I? That proves at least part of what I'm saying is true."

"How much?" she demanded.

"What?"

"How much, how much? How much do you owe him?"

Sighing, Shane bent down and wrote a number in the right column.

Jewel's eyes popped. "Forty-five thousand? You owe Cole fucking Waters forty-five thousand American fucking dollars? Are you insane?"

"It didn't start off that much," he protested. "It was only ten at the start, but…"

"Yeah, I'm sure," she said. "I know how guys like that operate." She rubbed her scalp through her long black hair. "Goddamn, Shane. Forty-five thousand dollars," she muttered. "You realize the only reason you're alive right now is that's his only chance of ever actually seeing any of that money again?"

"Oh, come on," he said. "Like I said, we go way back. We were kids together."

"Maybe so," Jewel said, "but this isn't kid stuff. Not by

a long shot. And what do you think is going to happen when he finds out you've got most of that money in hand and didn't immediately hand it over to him? And sure, maybe you and Cole ran around on the same playground or whatever the fuck, but you know who didn't? Me."

"Shit. Aw, shit." Shane's blood ran cold as he recalled his conversation with Cole earlier that day and the thump of the bus coming to a halt.

"Yeah, shit." Leaning forward, elbows on her knees, Jewel covered her mouth with her hands and moaned through her interlaced fingers, then covered her eyes and leaned back on the couch. "So even with this once-in-a-lifetime windfall dropping into our hands from nowhere, we're still nowhere near what we'd need to pay off our debts, let alone get on top of the situation. Fuck me," she spat, pouring herself more wine.

Shane looked over at Jewel, her lips screwed up in a cockeyed grimace. The thought that anything might happen to her as a result of his past mistakes was more than he could bear.

Suddenly, an idea popped into his head.

He almost blurted it out the moment it hit his brain, but instead he held onto it a few moments longer while Jewel sipped at her wine forlornly, turning it over and over in his mind. If anything, it seemed too perfect, too easy. And the problem was, he knew from hard-won experience that when any idea came to him easily, he almost always paid for it on the back end.

Still, they were out of options. He took the paper in his hands and did some quick mental calculations, then did them again. The math seemed right; if they got started the next day, the timeframe would work out. Sure, there were a few minor questions remaining to be solved, but nothing they couldn't handle—particularly with the benefit of a forty K bankroll backing them up.

And if anything was seriously wrong with the plan, surely Jewel would poke holes in it moments after hearing it, then mock him for ever bringing it up, and then they'd forget about it immediately anyway.

"What is it, baby?" he heard Jewel say. She was staring at him, expectation in her eyes.

He set the paper back on the coffee table and swallowed the dregs of his wine, then turned to her.

"I got an idea."

9798224489459